ISBN 13: 978-0-9824498-0-6
ISBN 10: 0-9824498-0-1
First Print July 2009
Printed in Hong Kong by Regal Printing Limited
On file at the Library of Congress.
1st Printing

Elephant, Elephant Come Alive!

Come Alive!

Written By
Steven P. Winkle

Illustrated By
Christie Mealo

Mystic Waters Publishing • Regal Printing Limited

Acknowledgements

The following people/elephants have contributed in outstanding ways to the creation of this book.

Mindy and Ricky Winkelstein, Howard and Matthew Markman, Kerry Lee MacLean, Richard Helfant and the Lucy Board, Jade Ariella Lien, Family, Friends, Teachers, The Pirate Stickers, and Lucy the Elephant.

Memory & Dedication

In Memory Of
Rose
&
Morty

I dedicate this and all of my work to the Ocean, which guides me, and to the Moon, which guides the Ocean.

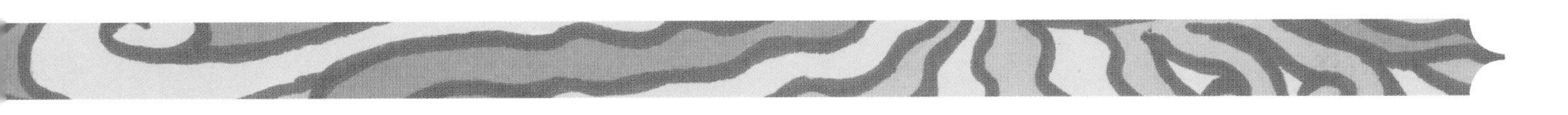

Sailing the sea of the Jersey Shore
The captain heard a shout!
A sailor in the crows nest bellowed,
His arms flailing about.

He wailed and moaned like a lunatic,
And on and on he went.
"I spot along the shore, my Captain,
A giant elephant!"

The sailors agreed he was crazy.
The captain thought him mad.
But of this man's very silly show,
The pirates were all glad.

None aboard the black-flagged ship a-sail
Believed him in the least.
And so they continued sailing north,
Toward a New York feast.

On the Isle of Absecon,

Living live as stone,

Was a lovely girl named Lucy,

Standing all alone.

She was, in fact, an elephant-

Giant as can be,

And people came from all the world,

Just so they could see.

She stood facing the east,

The ocean in her view,

And there she stays today,

So you can see her too.

Looming six tall stories,

Weighing ninety tons,

Almighty and impressive,

With a window in her buns.

Lucy was born many years ago,
In eighteen eighty one.
Over a hundred years she has lived
Beneath the yellow sun.

In all that time Lucy was content
To stand and face the shore,
But then one day the elephant knew
That she could stand no more.

She wished hard

With all of her elephant might

To break the magic

That bound her large legs tight.

And then came a voice,

"Revive, revive, revive!"

Singing,

"Elephant, elephant come **alive!**"

Imagine the surprise

Of all the Margate City folks!

They saw Lucy walking

And thought someone had played a hoax.

Oh, you should have seen them,

How the children screamed and laughed,

As they climbed into Lucy the Elephant's

Giant leg shaft.

Out a window in Lucy's belly,

And up onto the howdah,

The children scrambled, scaling Lucy,

Laughing louda' and louda'.

Lucy loved all the little children
Who climbed upon her back.
So, she blasted from her long trunk
A booming trumpet crack!

The entire city heard Lucy,
And knew it was no lie;
An elephant walked among them all,
Under the bright blue sky.

She stomped up Atlantic Avenue,

Near the beautiful beach.

When she reached the Margate Library,

She grabbed a book on speech.

The children helped Lucy read the book
Over one long, tough week.
By the end Lucy the Elephant
Had learned how to speak.

"Thank you, little children," said Lucy,
"For teaching me to talk."
The glad children said, "You are welcome!"
And went on with their walk.

Over to Ventnor Avenue
She took the good girls and boys,
And to thank them for all of their help
She bought them all beach toys.

And after that, they went to fill
Their big and little tummies
With Margate's famous Dino's subs,
The best of all the yummies!

Lucy ate a hundred subs
Before she stuffed her belly.
And when she burped the children said,
"Dude, that's pretty smelly!"

Lucy laughed, wiped her mouth, and said,

"It's time to go now."

And, as Lucy and the children left, they said,

"Thanks for all the chow!"

On they journeyed south and to the west,
Until they reached the bay side,
Where the Junior's Donuts & Dog's pier
Extended Margate's pride.

Lucy risked the planks with her great weight
As she stepped onto the pier.
But the wood boards held strong all along;
There had been no need to fear.

After a donut each for dessert,
They started off once again.
They traveled back toward the white beach,
Deciding to get shoes then.

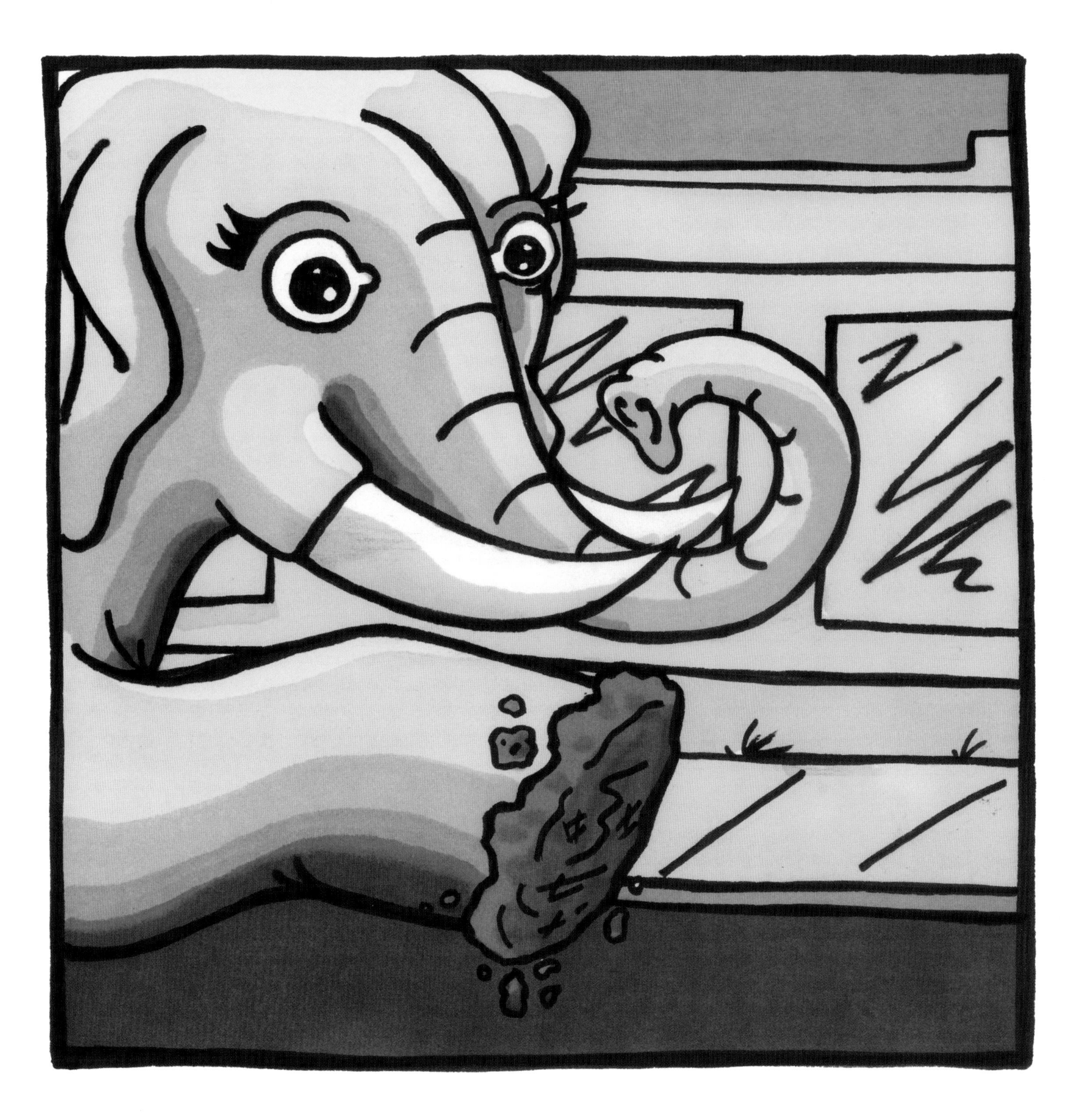

You see, Lucy's giant toes were bare,
And though her nails were painted pretty,
The bottoms of her humongous feet
Were getting rather gritty.

The children told the elephant,

"To Sassy of Margate for shoes!"

There, they knew, from all the coolest boots,

The elephant could choose.

When they arrived at Sassy Stacy's

She measured Lovely Lucy.

They found a pair of enormous kicks,

Which really were quite juicy.

"Thank you!" Lucy said,

And pranced in her new boots.

The elephant so happy,

Let loose from her trunk three toots.

Around the City of Margate
The elephant marched around.
Wherever she tramped
She caused a riotous sound.

When finally the sun was set
Lucy took the children home.
The elephant decided that she had
Used up all her time to roam.

With one last look around the little city,
Lucy waddled back to her home base.
She would miss all the friends she had made
While parading from place to place.

She sighed as she stood once again,

Looking out into the ocean.

And then Lucy was still, as if she had just drank

Some sleepy magic potion.

Trickling down one mighty elephant tusk
Was a single Lucy tear.
"Maybe," Lucy the Elephant thought,
"I will come alive again... next year."

Provided by Richard Helfant

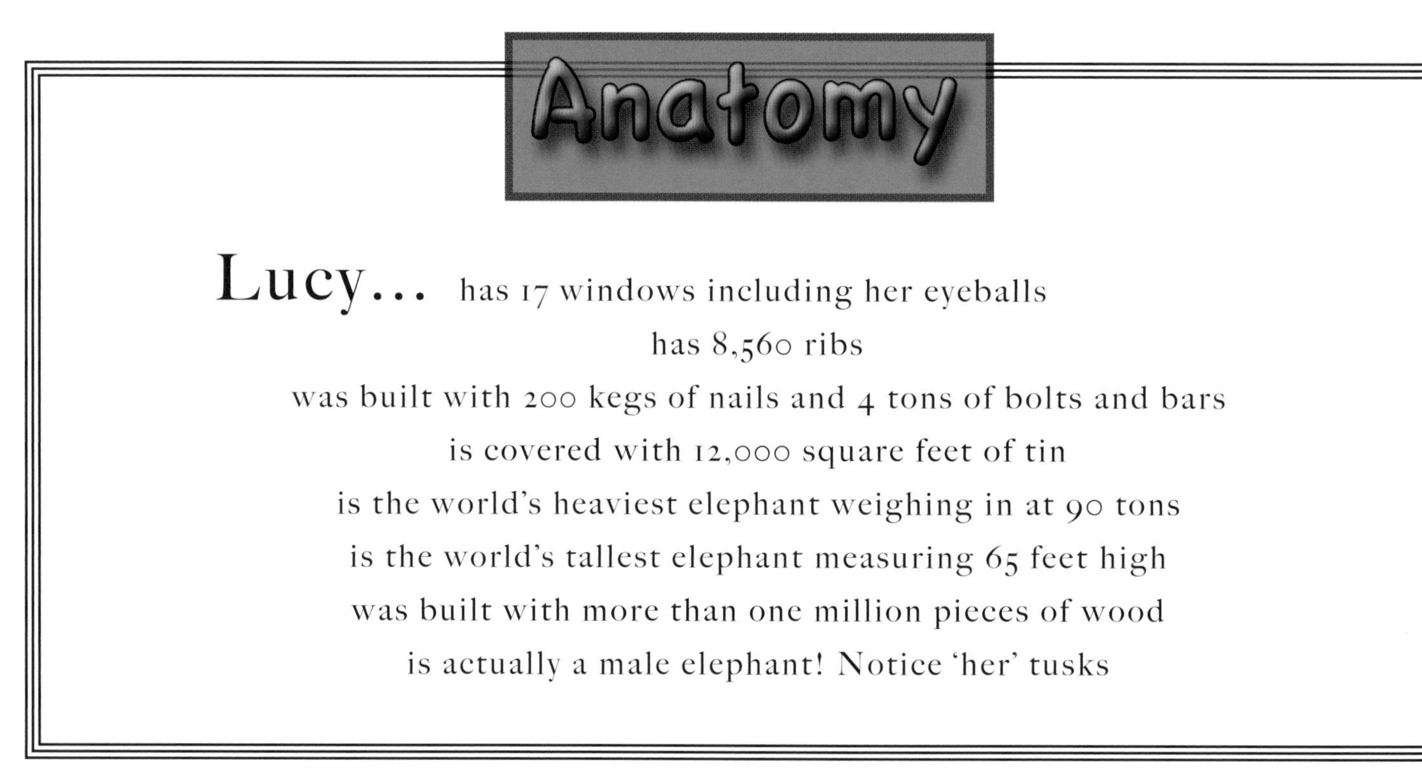

Lucy… has 17 windows including her eyeballs
has 8,560 ribs
was built with 200 kegs of nails and 4 tons of bolts and bars
is covered with 12,000 square feet of tin
is the world's heaviest elephant weighing in at 90 tons
is the world's tallest elephant measuring 65 feet high
was built with more than one million pieces of wood
is actually a male elephant! Notice 'her' tusks

Lucy… is the oldest example of Zoomorphic architecture in the world
Zoomorphic architecture is any kind of building
designed to look like an animal

Lucy… is also the oldest example of Mimetic architecture in the world
Mimetic architecture is any kind of building that
represents something from the natural world

PURPOSE

Lucy… was never a hotel
was a tavern
was a residence (home) for a physician (doctor) from England
was never a library

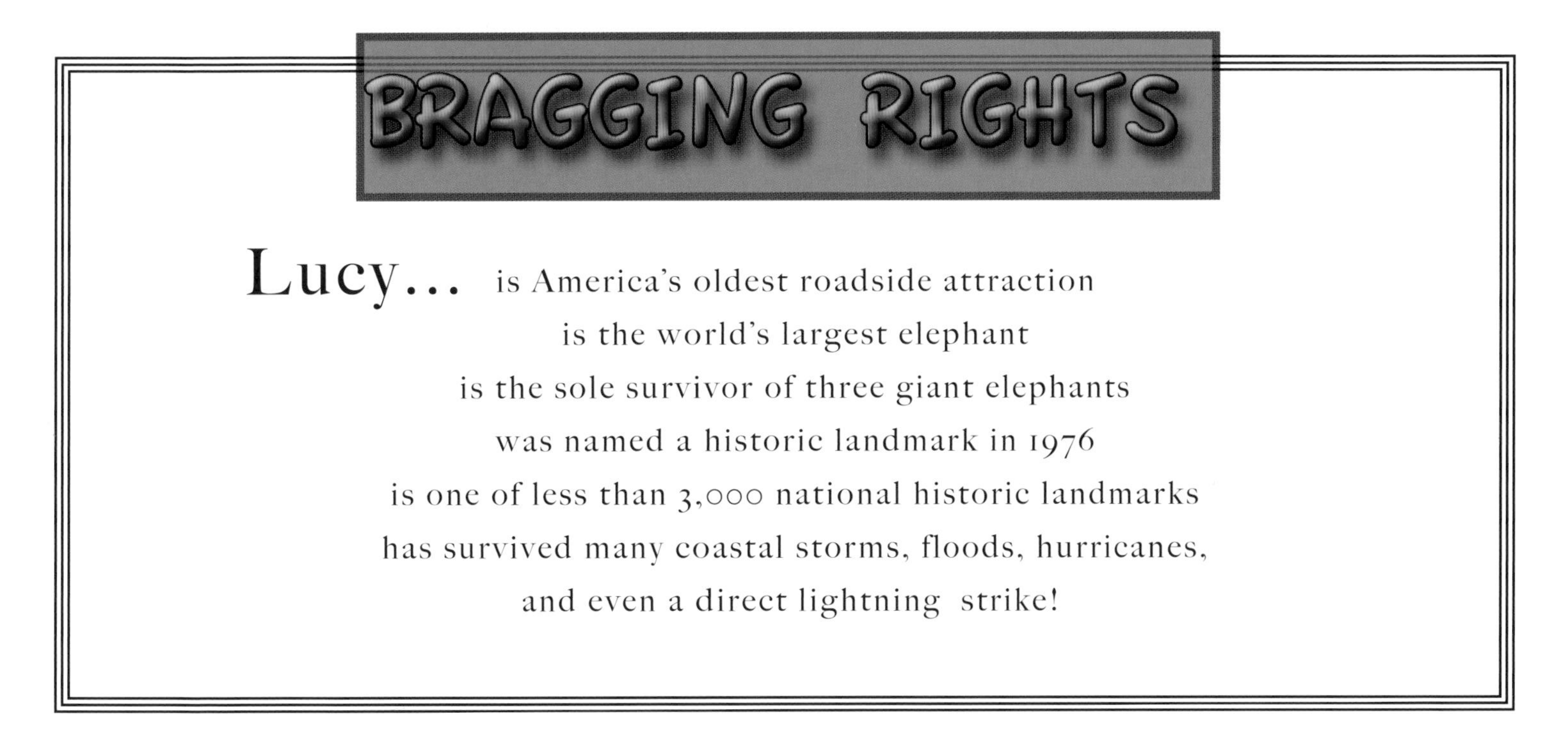

BRAGGING RIGHTS

Lucy… is America's oldest roadside attraction
is the world's largest elephant
is the sole survivor of three giant elephants
was named a historic landmark in 1976
is one of less than 3,000 national historic landmarks
has survived many coastal storms, floods, hurricanes,
and even a direct lightning strike!

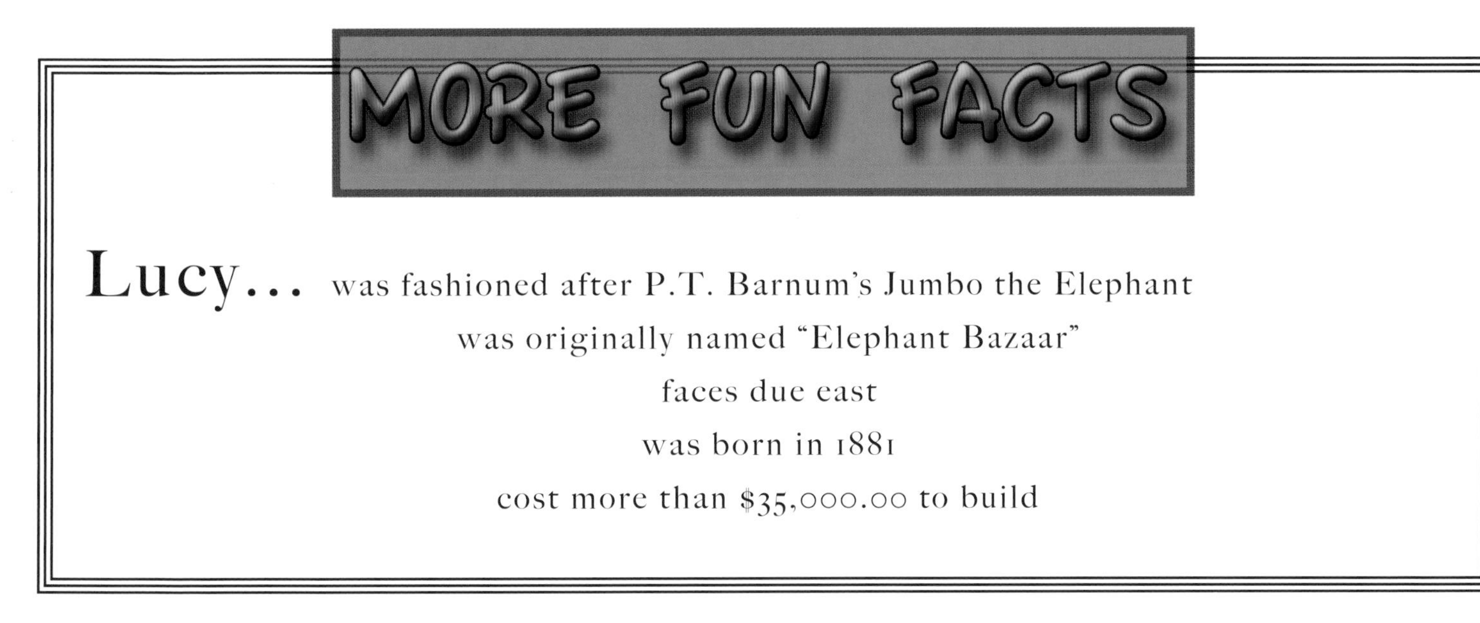

MORE FUN FACTS

Lucy… was fashioned after P.T. Barnum's Jumbo the Elephant
was originally named "Elephant Bazaar"
faces due east
was born in 1881
cost more than $35,000.00 to build